FAMILY DAYS OUT

Picnic at the Park

Meet the family

Priti

Alisha

Sofia

Mum

Dad

Logan

FAMILY DAYS OUT

Jackie Walter and Jem Maybank

Picnic at the Park

W

FRANKLIN WATTS

LONDON • SYDNEY

"Your dad's here, Logan!" called his mum on Saturday morning.

Logan groaned. He didn't want to go to his dad's new house, and he didn't want to hang out with Alisha and Sofia.

His dad used to spend weekends playing football with him. But since Dad had moved in with Priti, they had to do things that Priti and her girls liked to do as well.

"Hi, Logan, are you ready?" asked Dad cheerfully.

"Suppose so," Logan grumbled.

"Priti and the girls are in the car," said Dad.

"We thought we'd go
for a picnic in the park."

"Boring," thought Logan, but he said nothing.
"Have a great time. See you tomorrow,"
said Mum, kissing him goodbye.

Logan clambered into the back of the car.
"We're going to the park near
our house," Priti told him.

"It's brilliant – they've got a new zip wire and a splash park with fountains too," added Alisha.

Logan tried to smile. He knew they were being nice, but he didn't want to just go to the park. He wanted to play football.

"Everyone grab something to carry!" said Dad
as they parked.

Logan couldn't see a football in any of the bags.

"I bet Dad forgot it," he thought sadly,
as they passed a busy sports pitch.

They found a spot next to the splash fountains and set up for the day.

"Isn't it awesome?" Alisha said to Logan.

Logan had to agree that the splash park was fun. They all splashed as much as they could – even Dad and Priti got soaked!

"Who's hungry?" called Priti after an hour.
"ME! ME! ME!" they all cried.
Dad handed out some rolls. Logan wished they were his mum's sandwiches. At least he liked the watermelon they'd brought.

After lunch, Sofia had a nap. Alisha wanted to try the zip wire but Logan thought it looked rubbish. So Alisha pulled out her book. Logan didn't have his book. He wished his mum had packed it.

"Time for a kickabout?" asked Dad.

"You did bring a football!" grinned Logan.

"I thought you'd forgotten it."

"No way, it was the first thing I packed!" said Dad.

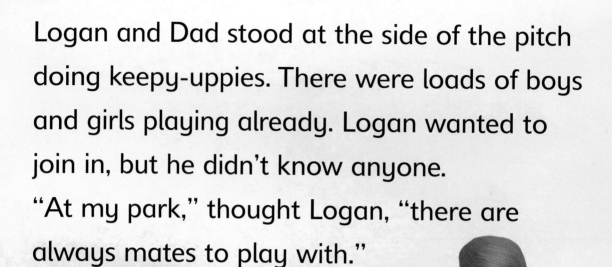

Logan and Dad stood at the side of the pitch doing keepy-uppies. There were loads of boys and girls playing already. Logan wanted to join in, but he didn't know anyone.

"At my park," thought Logan, "there are always mates to play with."

"Can I play?" It was Alisha.

"I suppose so," said Logan with a shrug.

"I didn't know you liked football."

"I'm on the school team!" said Alisha, laughing. "I reckon I'm better than you!"

"I know some of those kids from school,"
said Alisha. "We could play with them."

"Great," said Logan.

"Phew," said Dad. "I could do with a rest!"

Soon Dad was calling them back.

"Time to get ice creams," he said. "Maybe you could meet up with this crowd next time?"

"Both good ideas," said Logan, grinning at Alisha.

The ice-cream shop was next to the zip wire.
As he ate his ice cream, Logan thought it
didn't look that rubbish after all.

"What do you think, Alisha? Are you still up for the zip wire?" asked Logan. Alisha grinned.

Alisha and Logan went on the zip wire again and again. It was brilliant. But, at last, it was time to go home.

"Did you have a good time, kids?" asked Priti.
"Yes!" they all replied. Logan surprised himself
as he said it. He really had enjoyed it, after all!

A note about sharing this book

The Family Days Out series has been developed to provide a starting point for discussion about families and how these can be made up in many different ways. The series also gives children the chance to reflect on their own family life.

Each book emphasises the importance of spending time together, and shows how family members can support and help each other. The series encourages young children to learn to respect people's differences and treat all kinds of families fairly and without discrimination.

Picnic at the Park features a blended family with Dad and his son Logan, plus Priti and her daughters, Alisha and Sofia. Logan is reluctant to spend the weekend with his dad because he preferred it when he didn't also have to spend time with Priti and her daughters. He would rather play football with his friends near his house, but he ends up having a good time at the park near his dad's new home.

HOW TO USE THE BOOK
The book is designed for adults to share with either an individual child, or a group of children.

BEFORE READING THE STORY
Choose a time to read when you and the children are relaxed and have time to share the story.

Spend time looking at the illustrations and talk about what the book may be about before reading it together.

After reading, talk about the book with the children:

- What was it about? Have the children ever not wanted to go on a family day out? What happened? Did they end up having fun in the end?

- Ask: who are the people in their own family? This might include grandparents or other people who take care of them.

- Logan's mum and dad are separated, and Logan now has a new stepfamily. Ask: do you have or know anybody who has stepbrothers or stepsisters? What do you/they like doing together?

- Discuss where their family likes to spend time. Ask whether all the people in their family like going to the same places, or whether they prefer visiting different places. Ask whether there are places they do not like visiting with their family. This could perhaps be visiting the supermarket or going out to run errands.

- Discuss how their family makes this fair for everyone so that they all have a chance to do the things they like, and share the jobs they dislike.

- To encourage discussion, and help children who find it difficult to join in, you could play a quick-fire game of "Two Good, Two Bad".

ASK:
- What are the two best things you do in your family?
- What are the two worst things you do in your family?

You could note their answers down in a tally chart and use the results to make a bar graph about top family likes and dislikes.

First published in Great Britain in 2018
by The Watts Publishing Group

Copyright © The Watts Publishing Group 2018

Series Editor: Sarah Peutrill
Series Designer: Peter Scoulding

A CIP catalogue record for this book is
available from the British Library.

ISBN 978 1 4451 5898 3

Printed in China

Franklin Watts
An imprint of
Hachette Children's Group
Part of The Watts Publishing Group
Carmelite House
50 Victoria Embankment
London EC4Y 0DZ

An Hachette UK Company
www.hachette.co.uk

www.franklinwatts.co.uk

MIX
Paper from
responsible sources
FSC® C104740